# THE HUBBUB ABOVE

## Arthur Howard

HARCOURT, INC.

Orlando  Austin  New York  San Diego  Toronto  London

Requests for permission to make copies of any part of the work should be mailed to the following address:
Permissions Department, Harcourt, Inc.,
6277 Sea Harbor Drive, Orlando, Florida 32887-6777.

www.HarcourtBooks.com

Library of Congress Cataloging-in-Publication Data
Howard, Arthur.
The hubbub above/Arthur Howard.
p.   cm.
Summary: Sydney's new elephant neighbors make a lot of noise upstairs, but she does not mind as much after she is invited to their parties.
[1. Neighbors—Fiction.    2. Noise—Fiction.    3. Parties—Fiction.    4. Apartment houses—Fiction.    5. Elephants—Fiction.]   I. Title.
PZ7.H8283Hu   2005
[E]—dc22      2004007386
ISBN 0-15-204592-9

First edition

A C E G H F D B

Manufactured in China

The display lettering was created by Arthur Howard. • The text type was set in Parrish Roman.
Color separations by Colourscan Co. Pte. Ltd., Singapore • Manufactured by South China Printing Company, Ltd., China
This book was printed on totally chlorine-free Stora Enso Matte paper.
Production supervision by Ginger Boyer • Designed by Arthur Howard and Judythe Sieck

*A bedtime story
for the city that never sleeps*

$S$ydney lived way, way up
in a tall, tall building—
on the fifty-second floor, to be precise.
She loved it there.

She loved the ride in the elevator.

She loved the view from the balcony.

Most of all, she loved the quiet. Up on the
fifty-second floor, she couldn't hear the screeches,
the scrunches, or the vroom, vroom, VROOMS
from the street below.

*It's heavenly here,*
Sydney thought.

But then the Kabooms moved in upstairs.
They walked loud.

They talked loud.

And every Saturday night when they threw
a party, they cha-cha-ed very, VERY loud.

Sydney tried knocking on the ceiling.

She tried shouting from the balcony.

But nothing helped.

"Maybe you should move," said her Cousin Spike,
who lived downtown.

"Move?" said Sydney.
That did it.

It was time to pay the Kabooms a visit.

Mr. Kaboom opened the door.
He was very, very tall,
very, very wide,
and he looked a bit, well . . . tusky.

"I live downstairs," Sydney began. "And—"

"AND you're just in time for our party,"
said Mrs. Kaboom as she charged out of the kitchen.

What a party!
The food was awesome.

The band was hip.

And all the guests were party animals.

Cha-cha-cha, went Sydney.

CLOMP, CLOMP, CLOMP, went the Kabooms.

*That's* when Sydney remembered.

So when the band took a break,
Sydney took her hosts aside.
"This is the best party I've ever been to,"
she said. "But . . ."

And she explained as nicely as she could that
sometimes they walked kind of loud,
and sometimes they talked kind of loud,
and sometimes when they cha-cha-cha-ed upstairs,
everything downstairs cha-cha-*cha*-ed
right along with them.

"The trouble is," said Mr. Kaboom, "when you're
an elephant, sometimes a step can become a STOMP,
a clink can become a CLUNK,
and a bump can become a great big BOOM."

"But from now on, we'll remember to be quiet,"
said Mrs. Kaboom. "Really, we will. Because
you know, my dear, an elephant *never* forgets."

After that, the walking got a lot better.

And the talking got, well . . . a little better.

"And what about those parties?" asked Cousin Spike.
"You know, those loud cha-cha parties?"

"Oh, they're no problem," said Sydney. "No problem at all. Because, you see, the Kabooms *never* forget . . .

. . . to invite ME!"